P9-EIE-293

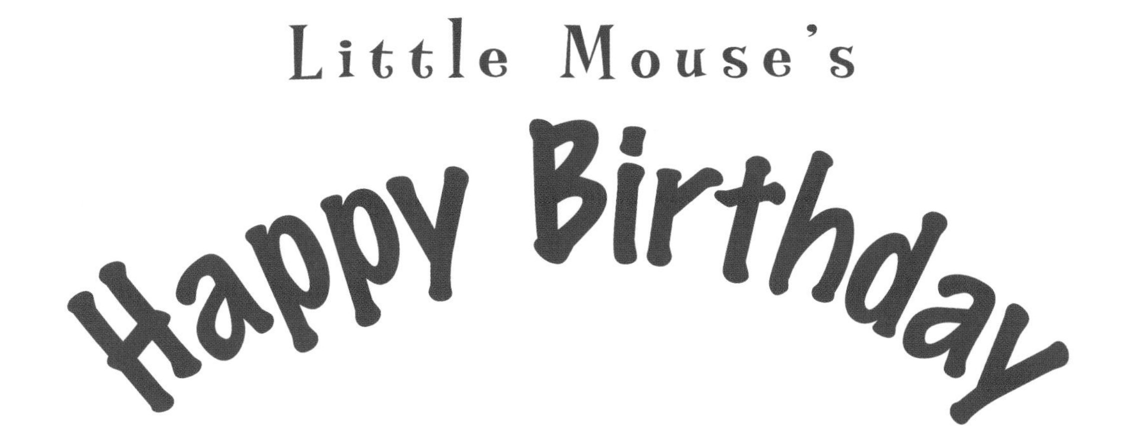
Little Mouse's
Happy Birthday

Little Mouse's

Happy Birthday

Jeanne Modesitt

Illustrated by
Robin Spowart

BOYDS MILLS PRESS
HONESDALE, PENNSYLVANIA

Boyds Mills Press, Inc.
A Highlights Company
815 Church Street
Honesdale, Pennsylvania 18431
Printed in China

Library of Congress Cataloging-in-Publication Data

Modesitt, Jeanne.
Little Mouse's happy birthday / Jeanne Modesitt ; illustrated by Robin Spowart. — 1st ed.
p. cm.
Summary: On her birthday, Little Mouse chooses to do things that will make other members of her family happy, which makes hers the best birthday ever.
ISBN-13: 978-1-59078-272-9 (hardcover : alk. paper)
[1. Birthdays—Fiction. 2. Family life—Fiction. 3. Mice—Fiction.]
I. Spowart, Robin, ill. II. Title.
PZ7.M715Lim 2007
[E]—dc22
2006020048

First edition, 2007
The text of this book is set in 18-point Optima.
The illustrations are done in colored pencil.
www.boydsmillspress.com

10 9 8 7 6 5 4 3 2 1

To Kyle Modesitt,
we love you
—J. M. and R. S.

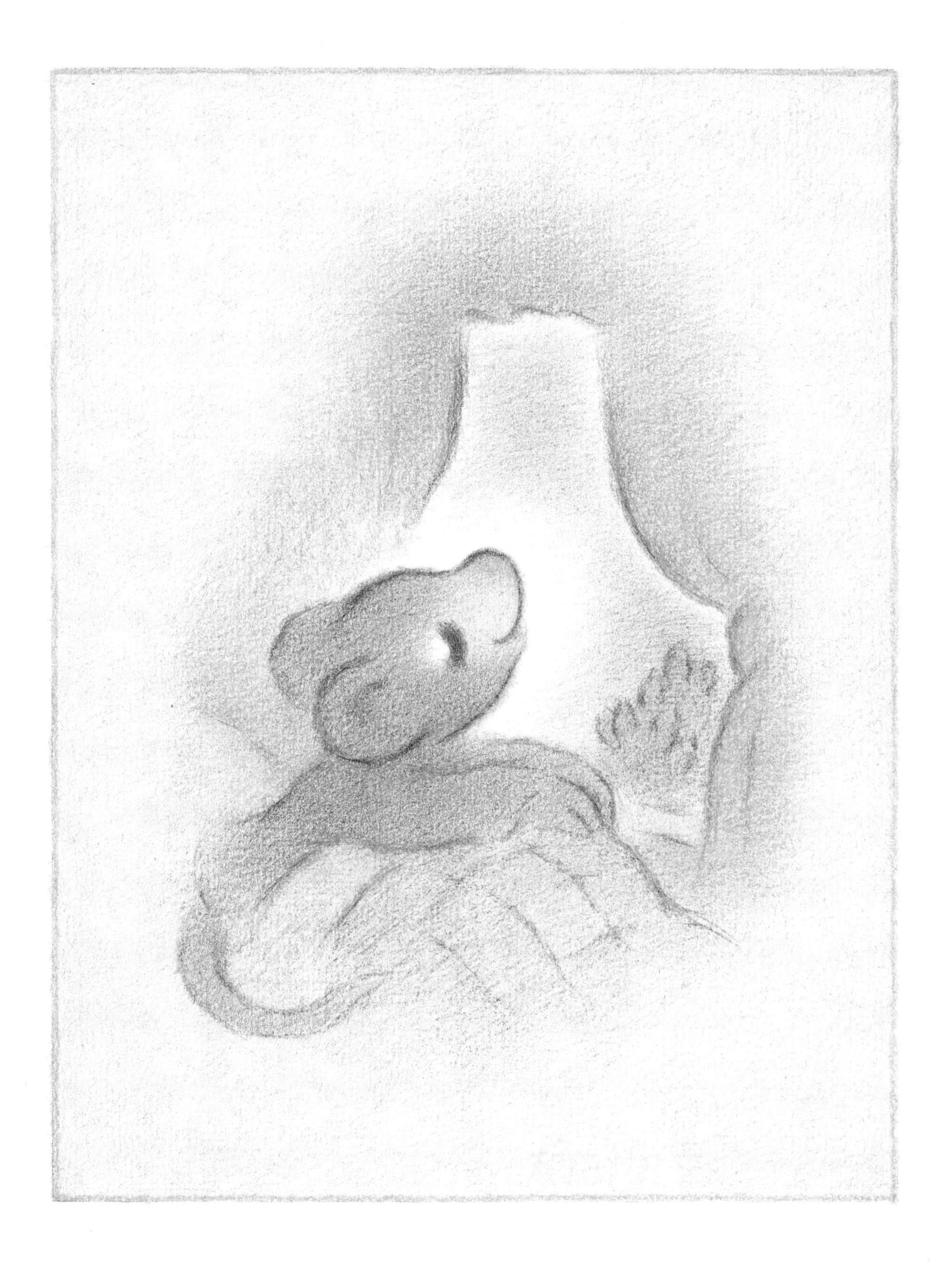

It was Saturday morning.

Little Mouse woke up and rubbed her eyes. Then she smiled. Today was her birthday! And she had a plan to make it the best birthday ever.

Just then Mama called from the kitchen. "Little Mouse, breakfast is ready."

Little Mouse hopped out of bed, washed her face, and put on her play clothes. Then she skipped into the kitchen. "Morning, everyone!" she said.

Papa, Mama, and Baby Brother looked up from the table.

"Morning, birthday girl," said Papa with a big smile.

Mama reached over and gave Little Mouse a hug. "Morning, honey," she said, "and happy birthday."

Little Mouse smiled up at Mama. "Thanks," she said. And then she sat down at the table and, with everyone else, began to eat.

When the family finished eating, Papa said, “Well, Little Mouse, today’s your day. What would you like to do?”

Little Mouse smiled. Now she could begin her plan!

“Well,” she said, “I’d like to go to the beach and build sand castles.”

Baby Brother jumped up and down. “Yippee!” he said. “I *love* building sand castles at the beach.”

Little Mouse grinned. She *knew* Baby Brother would say that. That’s why she picked it!

Sometime later, Little Mouse and her family were at the beach, building sand castles.

Everyone (especially Baby Brother!) was having lots of fun.

Finally, it was lunchtime.

Mama said, "Well, Little Mouse, where would you like to go for lunch? A restaurant, maybe?"

Little Mouse shook her head. "No, thank you," she said. "I'd like to have a picnic at the river."

Papa's eyes lit up. "Whoopee!" he said. "I *love* picnics at the river."

Little Mouse grinned. She *knew* Papa would say that. That's why she picked it!

One hour later, the family was at the river, eating a picnic lunch.

Everyone (especially Papa!) was having a wonderful time.

Finally, it was late afternoon. Papa said, "Is there anything else you'd like to do today, Little Mouse? Something special for this very special day?"

Little Mouse nodded. "I'd like to go to the meadow and fly kites."

Mama clapped her hands. "Oh, goody!" she said. "I *love* flying kites in the meadow."

Little Mouse grinned. She *knew* Mama would say that. That's why she picked it!

Sometime later, the family was in the meadow, flying kites. Everyone (especially Mama!) was having a splendid time.

At last, Mama said, "Well, dears, it's getting pretty late. I think we'd better head on home."

Everybody began to pull in the kites. Little Mouse looked at her family. Everyone was *so* happy. A big smile filled Little Mouse's face. *That* had been her plan: to make her birthday a happy day for *everyone*. And it had worked! Perfectly! Little Mouse felt so happy, she twirled on her toes.

A little while later, Little Mouse and her family reached home.

Little Mouse opened the door, and her eyes opened wide.

There, on the table, was the prettiest strawberry cake she had ever seen.

"Oh, yummy!" said Little Mouse. "Strawberry cake. I *love* strawberry cake!"

Baby Brother grinned. "We know," he said. "That's why we picked it!"

Little Mouse laughed, and she and Baby Brother skipped to the table.

It was, indeed, the best birthday ever.